The Bard Series

The Sapphire Knight

Michael Sullivan

Illustrated by Douglas Sirois

PUBLISHINGWORKS, INC.
Exeter, NH
2009

PublishingWorks, Inc.
60 Winter Street
Exeter, NH 03833
603-778-9883
For Sales and Orders:
1-800-738-6603 or 603-772-7200

Designed by: Kat Mack

LCCN: 200828968
ISBN: 1-933002-84-0
ISBN-13: 978-1-933002-84-2
Printed in Canada.

The Sapphire Knight

Other books by Michael Sullivan:

Escapade Johnson Series:

Mayhem at Mt. Moosilauke
Coffee Shop of the Living Dead
The Witches of Belknap County

All are available from PublishingWorks, Inc.

Contents

Chapter One:
The Knight and the Bard

The wind tore through my tattered cloak as if it weren't there. Winter caught me off guard—too far north and too far from anyone who knew me well enough to let me sleep in a protected corner of his barn. I was cutting across the heath when the flicker of a fire in the wind caught my eye. It was no more than half a mile away when I spotted it, so I knew it wasn't a large fire. Probably just a campfire of another lonely traveler.

Good, I thought. I wouldn't want to run across a group of revelers, or worse, a band of self-appointed witch hunters. Both could be dangerous to a stranger who wandered among them unlooked-for on such a night as this. Still, I approached the flames cautiously, until I saw just one huddled figure silhouetted against the firelight. Then, feeling it safer not to appear stealthy and suspicious, I stood back a distance and called out loudly.

"Good eventide, good sir. Is there room by your fire for hospitality?"

"Step forward lad, for a lad you be, despite your grown-up speech," came a voice from the huddled figure, deep and rich, but unmistakably old. "Your approach has been marked."

I looked about widely now, searching for sentries that might have noted my passing, but there was nary a soul upon the heath. I tentatively stepped into the outermost ring of light from the fire and realized my mistake. I was simply looking too high. A hound stepped from the darkness a moment after, close on my heels and silent as a shadow. He trotted easily past me and laid his chin across the crossed leg of the man at the fire.

Only then did the animal make a sound, a soft, comforting whine of companionship and devotion. A gnarled hand reached from beneath a heavy cloak and simply came to rest on the hound's head. "Take a seat, Friend, and warm yourself. No need to hang to the shadows. No one here will harm you."

I did as he told me, sitting on the ground opposite him, still feeling the need to have the fire between us. You cannot be too careful alone upon the heath at night, and the fact that this stranger seemed to have no cares at all could very well mean he was a danger himself.

Then I looked through the fire and into the face of age itself. Furrows ran so deep through his brow that they seemed to fall into themselves. His nose was bent too far to his right, and one eyelid drooped lazily to his cheek. But the other eye blazed so brightly it made the tongues of the flame stand out as shadows against its shimmering backdrop. I had seen my share of old people; living as a wanderer, I was always quick to seek out the old as being less likely to answer a plea for comfort with a kick. But I had never seen someone who wore age like a garment, a mantle that would seem to cover up a vibrant form beneath.

He must have noticed me staring, because he laughed out loud at my intensity.

"Young man, you look like you have seen a ghost. Have you never seen someone like me?"

"Not quite like you," I replied. "May I ask how old you are?"

"You can ask," he muttered, suddenly brought back to solemnity. "But you may not believe the answer. I am as old as time, if you count age in experience rather than years. I have seen the beginning and the end of the world, though I have walked this Earth for not much more than two score years and ten."

"Fifty!" I exclaimed aloud, before I could control my tongue. Ten minutes earlier, I would have thought such an age unattainable. Now, I would have guessed the man to be nearer eighty.

The old man seemed to read my thoughts, for he started to chuckle again. The sound was dry and crackled, but there was a spirit behind it—truth. When this man laughed, he meant it.

"Yes, it has taken only fifty years to turn me into what you see before you. The years have been hard on one such as me, and they have woven themselves into quite a tale, a tale fitting to a night such as this."

Despite my inborn cautiousness, I found myself leaning forward, my attention focused on the man before me, and the night seemed to have faded away. I always got this way when a storyteller, a good one at least, began to weave his tale. And this man was a storyteller of the first quality. His voice seemed to oil itself, loosening to the words like a rusty hinge becomes smoother with use. His voice, like his one good eye, was younger and more vibrant beneath the surface.

"Will you tell me?" I heard my voice ask, though I will swear that I never told my tongue to do so.

"I might," his eye twinkled, "if you can hear over the growling of my treacherous belly."

I stared blankly at him for a few breaths before the meaning of his words sank through the cloud that was forming around my head. As the light of consciousness returned to my eyes, his face broke into a wide grin. He nodded to the bag I had allowed to slide from my shoulder as I settled to the ground, and I realized he was asking if I had anything to eat, and whether I would share. He'd better be a wonderful storyteller, I told myself, if it will cost me provisions. Of course I had no choice but to share; I had invited myself into his company hoping to share a meal, only to find my host more desperate than myself.

I opened my sack and pulled out half a loaf of two-day-old bread and my treasure of all treasures, two fresh eggs. The bread I had begged honestly at the door of a poor farmhouse. The eggs I had exacted as penalty after being turned away empty-handed from a much larger and wealthier farm. Tightness from those so well blessed could not go unpunished. I couldn't resist a sigh as I handed over one of the eggs with a fistful of the bread. The old man seemed not to question the look I must have made, or the sigh, but his face brightened as he cradled the egg as if it were already hatched into a fragile chick. Then, with a snap of his wrist he loosed the golden yolk inside of it and popped one end of the shell with the nail of one thumb. In a second he had sucked the egg dry.

I attacked my egg with less skill and more deliberation, trying to draw the same pleasure from one egg as I had expected from two. All too soon, I held an empty shell in my hand. I crushed it, and fed the remains to the fire. When I looked up I thought I found the old man asleep, still sitting cross-legged before the fire, but slumped forward now with both eyelids drooping. Wonderful, I thought to myself, half my day's provisions gone and I don't even get my tale. There is gratitude for you. I laid myself down full length before the fire and pulled my cloak over me. As I settled my head on my arm, the old man's good eye suddenly sprang open, wild but unseeing, striving now with the flames before him. His voice came deeper, surer, smoother, as if it boiled up from deep beneath the Earth and found the old body a convenient fissure. Without preliminaries, he began his tale ...

Chapter Two:
The Sapphire Knight

I was a knight, you know, with land and a castle of my own. No, not a castle, really, but a small manor. I was the first son of a poor knight, and I inherited his station and property. More valuable was the training I received from the day I could first balance on my two feet. I could run almost before I could walk, and I could sit a horse almost before I could run. My father whittled my first sword right before my eyes, and it wasn't more than twice the length of a man's hand, but I wielded it with great honor at rats, hares, and even a few of the hounds my father kept and trained.

My father was not the type of knight who lounged around at court and played in tournaments and challenges. He ruled a small village and kept order; he trained his dogs and sold them to other knights, who had less skill but enough wits to know the value of a good hound. He married the daughter of a lord who had fallen into worse straits, being that his holdings were greater and thus took more to administer while producing less and less.

The one advantage the marriage brought my father was that when his sons, I the first of them, came of age, we were taken in as pages at the lord's service. There we learned the arts of war. In addition, we each learned a skill of use to the knight. I was given over for half of each afternoon to the priest who served the lord and his household. He was supposed to teach me letters and numbers so that I might one day take over my father's station.

But the priest was fat and lazy, and just appreciative enough of his great fortune to make sure I learned the basics of my lessons. Beyond that,

I was taught little in the time allotted, and if some days I failed to appear for my lessons, the greasy cleric simply slept away the hours undisturbed. On these afternoons, I could usually be found haunting the room of the lord's bard, listening to his tales and trying to commit as many to memory as I could.

One day the bard stopped in the middle of a story, trying to remember what came next, fingering his lyre absently, hoping the music would help him connect the lost ends of the string that tied the tale together. I waited just a heartbeat, then piped in with the next line. It was a story I had heard him tell many times, and had heard him sing in the great hall of the manor. He looked at me with open surprise and asked me what happened next. I finished the story for him while he sat looking at me with undisguised curiosity.

From that day forward, whenever I skipped out of my reading, writing, and adding lessons, the bard would tell me one story, and I would repeat back one of his. And if he was surprised when he found out I was memorizing his stories, he was even more so when I picked up his lyre and imitated the movement of his fingers over the strings. What came out was not to be mistaken for music, but with a few adjustments, the bard had me on my way to making real music to go with my stories. Before long, he began to pull out a flute to play while I was playing the lyre and singing my tales, and I learned to play the flute the same way as the lyre—by watching.

These happy years passed like water through a sieve, and I was far from tired of life as a page when I advanced to a squire with new and greater responsibilities, and more training in the craft of war. I enjoyed caring for the knights' horses and tending to their armor. I would gladly have stretched my years as a squire, before the time came for me to put on the armor of a knight. My lord was not a great lord, and my father was not a man of much consequence, so my knighting was no great event. I was presented before the king as one of a long line of young men, the look of whom made me wonder if I also looked so frail and scared.

The king did not even look at me as he laid the sword on my shoulder; he was deep in conversation with one of his finely clothed advisers and only paused long enough to say the few required words before returning to his conversation and moving down the line to the next kneeling figure. Why should he notice me? I was not likely to ever be before him again. My entire audience before the king lasted for less time than it would take to sing a hymn, and I was ushered out the door and to my duties back home.

So I returned to my father's house, and none too soon, as my father's health was failing him. He was ready to hand over the daily responsibilities of my inheritance immediately. The first night I was back in the family manor, he held a feast to which he invited the head of every family on his land, as well as his chief servants and all his men-at-arms.

To my astonishment, my father, whom I had seen only twice during the years of my training, announced to all that I was to take over the rule of his estate and lands immediately. He called to a servant, who brought out a new standard, my very own, and unveiled it before all. The meaning of the device on the flag was clear to all present, and was similar to the standards of my father and forefathers, yet different in a few distinct ways.

The standard was divided into four fields: two smaller ones at the top and two larger ones below. In the larger fields stood the stag, the symbol of a strong and peaceful family, and the golden spur that signifies knighthood. In the smaller fields above had been added a pen and a lyre, symbols of knowledge and contemplation that had not been on my father's standard. He had obviously kept abreast of my attainments in knowledge and music, and was telling me he was pleased. Most notable, though, were the colors.

The fields of my family's standards traditionally alternated between blue, signifying loyalty and truth, and white, for peace. Though trained as knights, and never slow to answer the calls of our lords and kings to battle, we had always been a family that wisely and peacefully ruled our little corner of the realm. On this, my standard, all the fields were a brilliant sapphire blue, separated by a thin ribbon of silver filigree. The effect was

startling, and the message clear. Peaceful we may be, but my career was to be marked by loyalty and strength. What my father saw in my future, or how he came to see it, I cannot say.

My life on my father's estate was no more exciting than life as a page, and less amusing. Ruling a small village is like picking up grain that is scattered in a yard. There are so many little details that the purpose seems unfathomable. Not only were there my own servants and my own fields to administer, but also the people who worked the farms on my land and looked to me as judge, master, protector, and chief entertainer.

All public celebrations were my responsibility, and such celebrations are a necessity, of course. Rule is not absolute, especially for a poor knight on poor land with many peasants and few men at arms. The successful ordering of life depends much on how well satisfied the peasants are, and how willing they are to offer their fidelity freely.

Any obedience that must be coerced is, in the long run, not of any value.

I quickly came to know the peasants and artisans who made up the little world over which I now held sway. I knew the ones who were jealous of their neighbors and would say anything to bring them down a little lower. I knew the ones who spoke with wisdom and had the most influence over the others. I knew which of the dirty children would steal a loaf from my very saddlebags if not watched, which ones would hide at the mere sight of me, and which could be trusted to carry a message or deliver some goods. Mine was not an estate rich with servants, and making use of the commoners was a necessity. I needed them as much as they needed me, and no amount of bowing and scraping could convince any of us otherwise.

That is why I was concerned when one spring morning, as I rode through the village, I heard of the strange malady that afflicted the daughter of one of the peasants. The girl was well known to me—a maiden of twelve summers who would one day make a pretty little wife to one of the village boys, but who for now was the joy of all by virtue of her sweet voice and merry airs. Most days there could be heard from her family's cabin her high, clear voice weaving verses of some old folk song. It was never a true ballad, but a celebration of the aroma of baking bread, or the taste of water from a mountain spring. On days when the villagers came together for some great work, be it threshing or raising a building or digging a dike, the girl was quickly relieved of any work and set to singing where all could hear and take heart. Her voice was a flower in a spring field, a band of stars on a summer evening, and the first snowfall of winter.

Her brother, some years her junior, brought me the news of her sickness. Her voice, he said, had run away, and her spirit was seeping away, going off in search of it. I could make no sense of the boy's description, and he was too sad and frightened to explain further. All he could do was beg me to come and make his sister better again, asked with the simple faith that I could do so with a command.

I came to the plain thatched house of the peasant and his family, and ducked to enter the low doorway. Little light filtered through the small windows cut roughly from the walls, but there was enough to show the single room, sparsely furnished with piles of straw for sleeping, a small table, and a hearth of fieldstones for cooking and heat. The peasant's wife knelt beside a pile of straw, bent over a slight figure reclining there. I stood behind the woman for some moments before she turned and looked up at me, her face stretched in pain and worry. She did not have her son's simple faith. She did not believe I could wave my hand and command her daughter to be well.

"What ails the child?" I asked.

"Sorcery," was the woman's simple, hopeless reply.

Chapter Three:
Scars

I started when I heard the old man use the word that meant fear and destruction in the country-side. I hadn't noticed how, as the old man wove his story, I had slowly risen from my lying position until I was sitting straight as a birch trunk, then leaning forward until my eyelashes were nearly singed by the fire. At the word "sorcery," I rocked back and lost my balance, landing in a heap against my bag on the ground behind me. The old man laughed.

I straightened up hurriedly, embarrassed that I had been so entranced by the tale, and angry at being laughed at. I summoned all the spite I could to cut him down a notch or two.

"Sorcery, was it?" I scoffed. "Was it the same magic that turned a knight into what you are now?

Or were you always like this, and the magic that made you a knight just wore off?"

I expected the old man to become angry. Liars like him usually hated being called out more than honest men would. But he did not become angry; his face made no sign that he had heard my remark. He reached a hand out absently to feed another stick to the fire and seemed to sink back into the past world he was remembering. But was he remembering a world that ever really was, or just one that existed in his old and withered mind?

"Were you really a knight?" I asked, immediately sorry for asking. If he truly had been a knight, my disbelief would be an unspeakable insult. If he had never been a knight, the question would look foolish and gullible. In the silence that hung in the air after the question had been spoken, I realized something else: If he had been a knight, and now was the lonely beggar who sat before this fire, exposed on a cold winter's night, some great tragedy must have befallen him that would be unbearable to think upon. If he had never been a knight, the elaborate drama he had invented might be the only thing holding his fractured mind together. Any way I looked at it, I had been wrong to ask.

I let a few seconds pass, then tried to cover over my words.

"Never mind that. What was really wrong with the girl? What happened to her? Go on, it's a great story."

"A great story," he repeated slowly, looking down into the fire. "Yes, a great and terrible story. But just a story? I wonder." He held a hand up before his face and turned it slowly, examining it closely as if he had never laid eyes upon it. As the palm turned outward, a flash of light from the flames showed in livid color the scar that ran across his palm, and the absence of the last three fingers.

Slowly, his eye rose to meet mine, and I could see he was falling back into his story. I settled back down across the fire from him, and his hound crept up closer, pressing his side into his master's leg. The old man's voice came once again from far away.

"Sorcery . . ."

Chapter Four:
Bird Song

Sorcery?" I asked, and I could feel myself recoil. I could defend myself against warriors, fire, wolves, and many other things, but magic was a foe you couldn't see, strike, or parry. Magic was the common enemy of all good people, and the peasantry was no more vulnerable to it than knights, or kings for that matter. But I quickly remembered that the fear of magic was an epidemic of the common people, and much more prevalent and dangerous than the real thing.

"What makes you fear sorcery?" I asked the woman. "Is this not some common illness?"

The woman's face turned to me with fierce determination. There was fear there, but anger as well—anger at the plight of her daughter and my disbelief.

"Her voice has been stolen. The music is gone."

I laughed then, in relief and at my own foolishness of shrinking from this sorcery.

"Why? She has lost her voice. 'Tis common enough. Odd this season of the year, but surely no work of evil."

The woman bowed her head submissively, but her voice rang out in defiance, an offense for which many a master would see cause for a beating, or worse.

"Her voice is not lost, it is stolen, I say. She has no pain in her throat, but a darkness creeps over her soul. She can speak, but she cannot sing!"

At that I was taken aback. The description of the girl's malady was odd, but the surety in her mother's voice was alarming.

"What do you mean she cannot sing? Is her voice weakened somehow, or is her mind turned against song?"

The voice that answered came not from the mother, but the daughter. It was soft and gentle, clear and steady, but without tone or sweetness.

"My mind wishes nothing more than to sing. I think I will die if I cannot. But the melody will not come, and the words have no rhythm. I simply cannot sing, and I am sore afraid."

I knelt at the girl's side and placed my hand against her forehead. She was neither feverish nor cold. Her face was pale, but her skin was not clammy. Her eyes . . . oh her eyes were dull, as if painted onto a wooden statue. I had never seen a person in such a state.

"But surely," I protested, "this is a matter for a healer to answer. There is some malady that afflicts you, child."

The girl gave no answer, but a single teardrop slid from one dull eye and her lips trembled. Her mother repeated the single word, "Sorcery," with a cold firmness, and I spun on her angrily.

"Stop saying that. It is fear that plagues this girl, and you are feeding it. Tell me why you fear magic afflicts her."

The woman gave no reply, but rose to her feet and beckoned me to follow her outside. In the garden behind the little house she stopped and crossed her arms defiantly. She looked at me expectantly, as if the answer to my question should be clear. I looked around and saw nothing out of the ordinary.

"What should I see?" I asked impatiently.

"What do you hear?" she replied flatly.

"I hear nothing." I was getting angry and less and less inclined to overlook the tone of this peasant woman toward her master.

"Exactly," she replied in triumph. "You hear nothing, and nothing has been heard in these parts for some days now. It is spring. There are trees all around. There are birds in the trees. Where are their songs?"

I drew a sharp breath and stared about me. Indeed there were birds all about, but none of them sang. None seemed to move for that matter. They sat on branches and stared dully into thin air. I spun my head around; no birds were outlined against the blue sky.

"They aren't nesting," the peasant woman stated, a touch of sadness seeping through her stolid bearing. "Not a single nest, not a single egg."

"How far?" I asked, hearing the tremble in my voice. "How far does this silence spread?"

"As far as I know of, but I have been much by my daughter's side. And it isn't silence; there are sounds, but all are crude and unpleasant. Dogs still bark, children still cry, but there is no music."

"Come," she commanded in a firm tone, one I suspect her husband heard from time to time, but one that she would never use toward me if her mind were not so clouded with worry. She led me down a path that led to the foot of a hill. She stopped before a spring that bubbled up to form a small stream and crossed her arms as before. This time I resisted the urge to demand an explanation, and let my ears explore my new surroundings. I could hear the stream, but something was wrong.

"It sounds harsh," I stated simply. The woman looked up at me.

"Streams sing, too, if you listen to them. This one doesn't."

"Sorcery," I said, and the peasant woman nodded.

Chapter Five:
The Healing Woman

The peasant woman pointed me to the healing woman's hovel, but refused to leave her daughter's side. I stood before the rundown collection of sticks and thatch that leaned precariously to the east, and realized for the first time that for all the people on my lands, this was the only place they had to turn when they were sick. No wonder the common people looked on illness as a hopeless curse.

I called out for the healer, but there was no reply. I stepped up to the doorway—just a rough hole cut in the side of a wall, covered by a stag's hide. I banged my fist on the wall once, and then held back in fear that a second blow would bring the whole structure down. I didn't need another knock anyway, for the door covering swung open a hand's breadth, and a dry voice wheezed out.

"Is that the master? Why the master it is, it is. You have waited long to visit old Hezekiah, yes indeed, a long time. I should have been called at the time of your mother's pain, and that was half a life ago. But now you come, and that is good. Hezekiah is waiting. Hezekiah will serve."

A wrinkled face, hardened and darkened by the merciless sun, emerged through the gap in the door. The old woman's head leaned forward in a submissive bow, but the eyes did not speak of submission. They stared cold and hard, rebuke flaring from beneath her wrinkled brow, even as a smile danced across her lips.

"You are the one they call the healing woman?" I asked.

"That is what they call me. Is there something that ails you, my master?" She leered up at me, and pointed a bony finger. "Or is there some improvement you wish to make? Some village girl you wish to enchant, perhaps. Not that a handsome young noble like yourself needs my poor skills, but perhaps there is something I can make . . . better?" She cackled.

I ignored her insulting tone and tried not to breathe the unwholesome air that rose from inside the hovel.

"Have you seen the maiden who has lost her voice, who cannot sing?"

The old woman's face went cold and rigid. "She has not lost her voice . . . it was stolen," she hissed, and she dropped the hide across the door.

Now I was not willing to overlook such discourtesy. I pushed aside the door cover and strode into the cabin. The stench nearly knocked me back outside. A smoky fire burned in the corner; an iron kettle hung on a ring above the flames, belching out greenish fumes. The carcasses of many animals hung from rickety rafters throughout the room, some still dripping blood into buckets. The old woman was busily rummaging through a stack of jugs, pointedly keeping her back to me.

"What do you mean, her voice was stolen?"

The old woman did not even turn, but she stopped feigning interest in her stores.

"I am speaking to you, and you will answer me!" My sword was out of its hilt and laid across her shoulder in a heartbeat, and with a little pressure, she was on her knees. Then she turned and wrapped her arms about my knees in supplication.

"Oh master!" she cried, her voice rising and shattering into shards. "Please do not make me interfere when evil is at work. My charms are no match for the Green Queen!"

"The Green Queen?" I asked. "I know of no such person. What land does she rule?"

"She rules the land that has no rule. She is master of a kingdom with no king. She commands thousands, and no man is her servant."

The old woman was babbling incoherently and weeping openly, a disturbing and disgusting form of sobbing that closely mimicked a wretch.

"Stop your riddling and tell me who this person is and how it is she could steal a young maiden's voice."

"She is a witch, my master, a sorceress of great power. She is called by many names, for she is as old as the forests that she haunts. Thus, she is called the Queen of the Green Wood. It is said that plants will not grow ere they ask her leave, and so she is called the Spring Queen or the Queen of May. In the old times, it is said, the ignorant would sacrifice to her to assure a good crop, even their children they would slay. If she could accept such a sacrifice, could she not steal a girl's voice? And who can say how the magical folk perform their deeds? Not poor Hezekiah, no, not poor Hezekiah."

"She is a witch, my master, a sorceress of great power."

I kicked her from my knees with disgust. "A moment ago, you offered to perform some magic on me; now you say this witch is harrying a young girl, and you don't know how. If magic is so evil, why do you practice it? Should I not tie you to a stone and cast you into the river?"

"No! No!" she screamed, and threw herself back on my knees, as if to drag me down with her to the depths if I should so punish her. "Hezekiah practices only the white magic, just herb lore and the reading of the stars. Hezekiah would never practice the magic of the spirits, no not so, not ever. Please, master, please."

And she dissolved into a heaving mass of rags at my feet. I looked at the carcasses hanging about the room, and could not help but wonder if some of the animals were unfit for food, even to such a wretch as this.

"Why do you think this Green Queen has bewitched the girl?"

"The White Lady," she replied, ceasing all sobbing and staring up reverently at a place a hand or two above my head. "The White Lady says that the Green Queen orders spirits about to do great mischief, and that Hezekiah must never call on spirits, but must become great in knowledge and know how to use this plant and that stone and to never use magic words or I shall become wicked like the Green Queen."

The words came out methodically and dully, a litany well-learned.

"Do you know why the birds don't sing, or the stream?"

The old woman's eyes went wide in genuine fear and horror. She shrank from my knees and fell back, half prone, to the dirt floor of the shack.

"The Green Queen has dominion over the birds and the beasts. The Green Queen is in league with the elements."

More litany. I clearly was dealing with a reflection of someone else's knowledge. I needed to get to the source.

"Where can I find the White Lady?"

"You do not find the White Lady. The White Lady will find you."

"I cannot wait for that. The girl's spirit is dying; anyone can see that. Where does the White Lady live?"

Confusion made the old woman's face a battlefield. Fears fought, advanced, and retreated against each other, contorting her features grotesquely. Finally, fear of the most immediate threat, the one before her holding a sword, won out.

"She lives beyond the great mounds, toward the foot of the mountains to the north."

"How far?"

"Hezekiah does not know," she cried. "The White Lady comes from there; Hezekiah does not go there!"

"What will happen to the girl? The one whose voice was stolen?"

The old woman's voice dropped even lower than mine.

"If she is under the sway of the Green Queen and her spirit magic, she will surely die. And she will not be the last." I turned and stalked out of the hovel. I had to return to my home. I had to get my armor and weapons of war. I had a journey to make.

Chapter Six:
The First Battle

I quickly gathered my gear of war. The fabric was of a bright blue, to match my standard and the device that had been painted on my shield. Plates across my shoulders and down my arms glittered in polished metal. All was fresh and new. I had used this gear only in practice and parades, and it was unmarred by battle. A servant spread a blue coat over my horse. The animal seemed to sense that something special was in store.

I was striding through the great hall of the manor when I noticed my lyre in a corner. How long had it been since I had played? Weeks? Months? I picked it up gently, as if it were a child, and ran my fingers across the strings. The sound that came from it had tones and notes, but they seemed broken and scattered in the air. They refused to fall into a rhythm.

It is spreading, I thought, and I hurried out the door. The groom had already hung my shield from my saddle and fitted a spear in place. I swung up into the saddle and galloped off, my horse waiting for no prompt, excited to be under way. Although I hadn't ridden him as much as I should have in preparation, he seemed sturdy and strong, and the ground shook under his massive hoofs. The people of my lands stopped and turned, keen with interest and wonder, to see their master riding off in such a martial manner.

The feeling of parade faded as we rode past the edges of farmland and into the wild country to the north. A series of high mounds, or low hills, formed a border between the land I had always known as my father's and a country where he, and supposedly no other lord, held sway. Crossing through that barrier left me feeling weak and exposed.

Bandits, I told myself; I am just afraid there might be bandits. But that was not really why I felt so strange. Surely there were bandits about, and a band large enough might attack a solo knight, but I knew that bandits themselves had no love for the wild lands.

After the initial dash, my horse settled into a trot for many hours of the afternoon. The ground was difficult and uneven, so the traveling was slow, but we came through the last of the mounds just before sunset. There, some leagues away, but clearly outlined against the darkening sky on the first of the mountains to the north, was a splendid-looking castle. Four spires rose majestically above a surrounding wall that, even from a distance, looked immense. The path to its gate was clear up a rising slope. But the distance was too great to be covered before dark, so I camped for the evening on the very edge of the wilds.

After driving a stake in the ground and hobbling my horse to it with a length of rope, I gathered wood for a fire. I broke into the stores I had put up in my saddlebags. The wind came unbroken here on the northern edge of the mounds, and I realized how cold this land could be, even in springtime. Huddled in my cloak, on the southerly side of a roaring fire, I gazed up at the towers of the White Lady. They were imposing and formidable, giving out an air of solidity and security. That seemed a grand thing on the exposed plain that led to the feet of the mountains. The night was still; not an animal seemed to be rustling in the brush; no wolf howled in the dark. I slept deeply till the rising of the sun.

In the morning, I saddled and loaded my horse, and started up the last stretch to the stronghold of the White Lady. As the road rose to meet the imposing gate, the trees thinned, then disappeared. The brush became more and more scarce until it too ended. In the final stretch, there was nothing on the landscape except beautifully kept grass covering a final stretch of less than a league of flat plateau.

At the edge of this expanse, I stopped to survey a grim scene. A path of worn ground led in a straight line toward the fortress before me, and an enormous structure of stone laid on stone rose to a greater height than any I had ever seen. Indeed, two of the lord's castles, stacked one atop the other, could not have reached such a height. The walls appeared to be absolutely smooth, as if the stones themselves had been taken from the bottom of the sea. All was limed a bright white that flashed in the sun.

Still, it was not the fortress that startled me, but the ground that lay before it. Suits of armor were scattered all about the worn path. Some appeared empty, as if discarded, but others told the true tale. Knights in various stages of disintegration lay all about, exposed to the scavenging beasts, slowly leaving the shells of their own armor. Shields and weapons, enough to make a vast armory, rusted in the open air.

Perhaps more disturbing were the bodies of a few horses, skewered by lances and lying about. No knight of honor would strike a horse in a challenge. Knights left unburied to rot on the field, horses lanced, something beyond my reckoning had happened here.

At the end of the path stood, motionless, the tallest and most formidable knight I had ever seen. Even at that distance he looked impressive, and I knew that at close range he would be easily twice my size. The horse he sat upon was as still and solid as he, well proportioned to its rider, and the size of a peasant's home.

It dawned on me then that I was looking on a statue. No man, or horse, could reach such size or stand so still. Surely this was not the real danger, just a stern warning.

I was wrong.

I urged my horse forward a few paces, and suddenly the knight opposite me lowered his lance into position, pointing directly at me. My horse's mane bristled and his muscles tensed, but he held his ground. I reached for my lance and fit it into place. But no challenge came from my opponent, and he made no move. He stood as impassive as he had before. I looked at the fallen foes about and wondered how many others had simply fled at so clear a challenge. I imagined myself flying before this, my first battle, and the shame I felt at the thought strengthened my resolve.

I looked down at the sapphire-colored shield I bore, and the memory of my father's bestowing came to my mind. Peaceful we may be, but strength and truth would mark my way in the world. I set my heart on finding the truth behind those tall white walls, and on proving myself worthy of my armor.

I sat forward in my saddle and called out loudly to the great knight before me.

"I mean to pass. I have need of speech with the White Lady who lives within. Will you let me pass?" No answer came from the knight, nor did he make any move.

"I have no love of war," I called out. "I simply wish to pass. May I pass?"

Again, there was no answer. The thought of those defeated knights left scornfully in the open to be the prey of birds and wolves now began to burn my mind with anger.

"Good sir knight, this discourtesy is unbecoming. If you mean to bar me, say you so. Stand not so still as the stones you guard!"

Silence met my words, and as I became angry, fear faded.

"Perhaps you are no knight, certainly not one of any honor, you who stand so arrogantly. I come. Bar me if you will."

I spurred my horse forward, first one step, then another. No response. We broke into a canter while the knight looked on. Suddenly, the other knight's horse broke forward, charging down the beaten path. The sound of his coming was like that of a tearing wind grinding down a forest, yet it seemed to move effortlessly. The knight gave no yell, no war cry; he rode high in the saddle as if unconcerned with what he might meet.

My horse, suddenly recognizing the action that he had practiced so often in training, broke into a charge without waiting for a signal from me. He was well trained, but lacked experience, and at full charge he lost his footing. His knees buckled and he pitched forward, tossing me high over his head. For a moment, I felt like I hung in the air, as defenseless as the targets that knights-in-training picked off with ease as the objects were tossed up before them. A slight rise of the lance, and I would be spitted like a wild boar to be roasted over a fire.

To my amazement, the lance did not rise, but bore down where I had been. My stumbling horse passed just under its tip, and I flew above. I had just the wits to brace myself before my own lance drove high into my opponent's chest and splintered wildly. The force of my flight, with the speed of the onrushing knight, created a fearful impact. The other knight's breastplate collapsed, his helmet flew off, his whole body flew backwards, and I flew over him. I hit the ground and knew no more.

Chapter Seven:
The White Lady

I awoke to find myself staring up at a clear sky, my horse nudging my face. I lifted myself to a sitting position, and except for a headache like none I had ever had, I seemed to be in one piece. The shattered remains of my lance lay scattered across many yards of ground, and in the center of the circle of debris lay the great knight I had battled. He was laying in a heap, unmoving, limbs and head jutting out of his torso at some exceptional angles. Still, I was cautious as I dragged myself to my feet and drew my sword. I approached the prone figure, but the knight did not move.

I reached out a toe and tapped the head. To my shock, it rolled clear of the body! I turned away in disgust, and then realized that I saw no blood, no gore. In fascination, I looked more closely. From the shoulders of the knight protruded an iron bar. The head was carved wood, cunningly shaped and painted to appear lifelike. It was then I noticed the enormous warhorse, standing as still as a statue, still facing down the path to where I had come from. Its hind legs rested, not on the ground, but on long wooden beams that stretched back to the very gates of the castle. I found the front hooves suspended a hand's breadth above the ground, as if the horse were frozen in a forward leap. The entire horse was carved from a dark wood and encased in shining metal.

All this proved too confusing for my mind to comprehend, and I went back to the figure of the knight to make a closer examination. I pulled back the cloak that ran along its shoulder to find a carved wooden form in several pieces covered by plate armor. The right arm was a piece separate from the midsection, ending in a great ball that fitted into a cavity of the torso, and so could move up and down between two blocks that clearly marked the lance being up and it being down. The feet were wrapped in leather thongs that had once held the knight in his saddle, but now were torn and shredded.

Not a knight at all, I thought, but some moving statue of a knight. That certainly explained his great size and the enormity of his horse, and why so many vanquished knights had been left to rot in the open. This unfeeling warrior would feel no pain, no fear, and no sense of duty towards his foes. It was there to destroy knights, not to bury them. It also explained why so many had been defeated. This knight was so much bigger and heavier than a human knight, his horse more powerful and less fearful than one of flesh and bone. But how did it move forward with such speed? The answer to that question, and the goal of my quest, both lay

"Not a knight at all, I thought, but some moving statue of a knight."

somewhere behind the walls of the White Lady's castle. It was there that I turned.

I took the reins of my horse, a bit lame from his stumble but otherwise unscathed, and led him up to the gates. My sword being still in my hands, I banged on the wooden gate with the hilt. The gates swung open, though none could be seen to work them. I stepped through into a broad courtyard, and froze.

Arrayed before me were some two score knights, all huge, all atop mountainous warhorses, staring right at me. No, I thought, not *at* me, but *above* me. They all sat impassively, staring straight ahead from their great height. More statues, I thought, but if they can all move then I am in great danger. I snuck a glance at the ground. Each stood at the front of a wooden beam that in turn sat in a long groove that led out the gate and met with the groove that marked the trail of the knight I had defeated.

I quickly stepped aside until I was clear of these grooves. I then watched in fascination as the wooden beam that had pushed the knight recoiled back through its groove and came to rest in an empty spot in the line. Slowly, one of the other knights rode forward to the sound of wood and metal grating against ground. He passed through the gates and stopped just before them. The gates swung closed.

From where I stood, I could see wooden beams reaching back from the knights to great wheels standing straight as pillars. One of them turned slightly as the replacement knight took his place and settled with a click as some unseen working found its proper place. I was fascinated. I was also frightened and confused. What purpose could such a machine serve? Who was operating it? I could see no one turn the wheel. I was pondering these questions when I heard a clear, crystalline voice that seemed to come from all the walls of the courtyard at once.

"Congratulations, Sir Knight. You are the first to ever defeat my champion. You are clearly brave and powerful. You are worthy, and you are welcome."

The voice was perfect in tone, flawless and sure, but it was flat and unmusical. I could not find its source. I answered, speaking into the open air.

"And why did I have to win this battle? Why attack me without provocation?"

"A test," returned the glassy voice. "Not everyone is worthy to stand before the White Lady. But you are a knight like few others, so I grant you an audience and the favor of doing my bidding."

"I am not inclined to do the bidding of one who has taken me for an enemy. Instead, I would ask the favor of your knowledge. The healing woman in my village says you know of the Queen of the Woods."

The voice changed slightly; it sounded just a bit more insistent.

"Indeed, I know of the Green Witch and her evil doings. What do you have to do with her?"

"She has stolen something from my village . . ." I hesitated, unsure how I would sound if I told the story that the simple village women had told me.

"She has taken the music." The crystal voice was now calm again. It was not a question.

"Yes," I replied, both relieved and surprised at her knowledge. "The women of my village think that you may have the magic to oppose her."

Now the voice turned cold. "The simple of this world put their faith and trust in magic, and while I can command magic, you see that I choose a better way. There is no magic in my defenders, only what is real and natural. But I have the weapon to oppose this menace. Indeed, I have seen her downfall— and it is you. You have come here to be my arm, to carry my sword against my enemy and rid the world of her and her dark arts forever!"

"I serve a lord and a king already, and wish for no new master, but if your ends and my own are in accord, I will welcome your aid and offer my own."

"Then step forward, and take my aid from my own hands." A section of the stone wall before me swung open noiselessly, and a great light shone forth from it. From that light stepped a stately woman dressed all in white, with hair so white it spun colors from the light that radiated from behind her. Her face was fine and carved; her shoulders too could have been chiseled from stone. Her head was held high and as unmoving as one of her knights as she stepped forward into the courtyard.

"Pledge to me that you will destroy this sorceress, and I will give you a weapon against which no enemy may stand."

"I pledge to do my all to rid this world of all wickedness," I replied, and my voice sounded strangely bold and powerful as it echoed off the high stone walls.

"Then take this sword and bear it well." She lifted from the folds of her gown a flashing blade and held the hilt out to me. I was amazed at how light it felt as it settled in my hand, as if it were made of a thin strip of wood. I looked closely and saw that the blade was long and thin, its two edges running down from a ridge that ran the entire length. At the edges, the metal was a sliver; it would pass through flesh like a knife through soft bread.

"What sorcery spawned this?" I asked in amazement.

"The marriage of metals," she replied in a hushed tone.

"Alchemy," I whispered, and for a moment we were both silent, in awe of the mystery before us.

"This is the Sword of Days to Come. No blade can stand against it. It is light to swing, but harder than any armor. Defeat the Green Witch,

and the fame of this weapon will be matched only by your own."

I stood entranced by the light that seemed to leap from the blade, and by the bright image the White Lady painted of my success, which seemed so sure. But then my wits returned to me, and I remembered the mission on which I had come.

"Tell me—for you clearly see much and understand far more than I—why does the sorceress in the woods steal music from my people, and how? If I must challenge and defeat her, I must know."

"Who can understand the purposes of one so wild? She lives in darkness; her thoughts are dark. She communes with wild creatures; she is avaricious and uncivilized. Things that hide in the dark woods must be dragged out and destroyed, it is ordained. But her power is old, and the woods themselves defend her. She gives dominion over the affairs of men to the beasts of the field and the birds of the air. Attack her realm without mercy if you wish to defeat her."

Of this, I understood nothing. I knew only that here was an ally willing to aid me in my quest, so I accepted her sword and turned to go. As I reached the gates, they seemed to open of their own accord, and I went forth from the stone castle with the great Sword of Days to Come in my hand. I stepped up into the saddle and rode off toward the dark wood.

Chapter Eight:
The Dark Wood

My heart was troubled as I rode back down the slope of the hills into the green valleys below. The magnificent sword felt light and nimble in its sheath, and I had an ally against the sorceress that I had been warned was plaguing my village. Still I felt uneasy. Perhaps it was knowledge that I was about to enter the heart of the great dark wood, a place where even the bravest hunters did not venture. The great stags seemed to know this, and when chased would often run for shelter in the darkest glades.

Perhaps it was fear of the great magic that lay within the green wood that made me hesitate. I had all but breathed in a fear of magic since I was a boy. Magic was a mystery that filled the air around my village, and maybe all villages. It was tolerated in small doses, and left to those who would coax it to whatever benign purpose they could. Such people, like the healing woman, were not honored, but pitied and feared. Contact with magic was a contagion, and those affected were quarantined and avoided.

The barren landscape gave way slowly to scrub grass, and then to scattered forest. I rode a circuit around the sparsely settled lands on the outer edges of the village and camped for the night on the outskirts of the last field of the land I knew from my boyhood. In the morning I checked my stores and saddled up for the plunge into the dark wood.

The canopy of trees closed in above me, and the path narrowed. I saw the sun for the last time when it reached its zenith, just before the boughs met and closed off the sky. The gloom darkened steadily. I don't know how late was the hour when I stopped for the night; the setting of the sun only changed the degree of dimness around me. I tossed beneath my cloak that night, unable to clear my mind of the images that I had seen, of the lifeless knights that charged with terrible intent, of the pretty little village girl, her eyes full of terror and loss, the skulking figure of the healing woman over her sordid supplies, and the proud and cold White Lady in her stone castle holding out the glittering Sword of Days to Come.

Just before a dim dawn broke, filtering through the roof of leaves, my feverish dreams showed me the figure of a fawn stepping lightly through forest undergrowth. It paused, looking down where I lay, with a look so trusting and secure I felt at an instant that no harm would come to it. Very slowly it lowered its head to mine and whispered the words, "You may come."

With a bound, the fawn was off, and I shook myself awake, sitting up and imagining I saw a waving of branches where the fawn had disappeared into the undergrowth. Magic, I thought, is all around me now. I can feel it on the breeze; I can taste it in the air. It oozes from the bark of these ancient trees. I shivered despite the closeness of the warm and heavy spring air, here protected from the chill winds that buffeted the plains where the White Lady dwelt.

The path held, though it was a twisting line now, barely wide enough to admit the bulk of my horse, and I lay flat atop its neck for fear of a tree limb taking me from my saddle. I was so intent upon keeping my place that I did not see the end of the path as I emerged through the trees, but found myself suddenly in a clearing the size of the great room in my father's manor. The sun poured through an opening in the canopy of trees. My horse came to a sudden halt, standing rigid as stone, indeed as solid as the horses of the knights that guarded the White Lady's castle. Before us, in a half circle, stood a pack of wolves, teeth bared, crouched and ready to spring.

Though they didn't move against us, it was immediately clear to me that these were no animated statues. The hair bristled on the wolves' backs, their muscles twitched, and I was close enough to see their eyes blink. I tried to urge my horse backwards toward the path, but a deep-throated growl made me turn to look behind me. Standing on his back legs, his head almost level to mine, was the largest black bear I had ever scene, hind paws planted in the entrance to the path. I was trapped.

There was nothing left for me to do but draw my sword. The magnificent weapon pulled noiselessly from its sheath and announced its presence to the world by a flash of reflected sunlight that sent splashes of color into all the shadows about the glade. I felt a thrill run through me, as the power of the sword seemed to fill my veins. I was invincible.

Before I could make my first thrust, though, a voice lifted my thoughts from their reverie and made me pause. The voice was light, airy, full of sunlight and stars, and borne on the very breeze. It carried no command, only an invitation to listen and be at peace.

"Hold your hand, good Sir Knight, or you will spill innocent blood, and that is forbidden here. You shall regret your rash act for many a long day."

At the sound of the voice, I could feel my horse relax. His head dipped, and he no longer half-reared from the wolves before him. The wolves, too, relaxed on their haunches. The bear lowered his paws and looked at me somewhat quizzically. I suddenly felt foolish for brandishing a sword in what was, to all appearances, a peaceful, bucolic scene. I sheathed the sword, and immediately felt the tingling in my spine that occurred whenever I believed I was in the presence of something unnatural. Was this sorcery? Had I just lowered my defense at the enchantment of an enemy?

As if in answer to my thoughts, a young woman stepped through the half circle of wolves, running her hands along the heads of two of them as she passed. She was dressed in green from head to foot, from her mantle of soft cloth to her slippers of silk. Her clothes were unadorned, but they seemed to shimmer in the sunlight. Her face was that of youth itself, fresh and full and smooth as a lake at sunset. She was the picture of youthful beauty on a spring morning.

She stood before my horse and rubbed his nose playfully, wearing a smile that glowed from within. For a moment she seemed lost in a world that included only the great steed and herself. When she looked up, she seemed surprised to see me.

"Sir Knight, is this horse with you? But of course he is; there you are astride him, and a lovely

"Her face was that of youth itself, fresh and full and smooth as a lake at sunset."

animal he is. Do you think he likes clover?" And she was spinning off a few feet to a clover patch in the clearing. In a flash she was back, holding a bunch of the leaves beneath my horse's nose.

"He does like clover! How wonderful! He shall have his fill. Would you like to see the butterflies? They have gathered just at the other side of the clearing and are doing the most delightful dance."

My head clouded at this seemingly pointless chatter, and I had to shake my head to clear it. Enchantment, I was sure, meant to put me off my guard. I spurred my horse to rear up, as much to stimulate myself to action as him, but he simply ignored my prompting and kept munching the clover from the lady's hands. If I didn't know it to be impossible, I would swear he was smiling at her.

That convinced me. I knew now that I and all the creatures about me were under a spell. I leapt from my horse and once again drew the shining sword given me by the White Lady. I was ready for the wolves to charge, for the bear to attack, and especially for the girl in green to wave her hand and produce a light to strike me with. None of these things happened. To my surprise, the girl began to cry.

Chapter Nine:
The Queen of May

No assault could have left me more disarmed. The sword in my hand seemed to cry out to strike, but my arm would not move. The wolves, the bear, even my horse seemed to look sorrowfully at the young woman, more beautiful in sorrow than she had been in her joy. The trees themselves seemed to weep with her. I stood frozen in confusion. It seemed that half the day had passed before I could move, and then I simply lowered my sword.

"That blade," the young woman said, in a tone that was lower but no less sweet, "that blade comes from the Lady in White, does it not?"

"It does," I replied. "She calls it the Sword of Days to Come. She has given it to me to aid my quest. Are you the mistress of this wood? The witch they call the Green Queen?"

"I am known by many names, the Mistress of Spring, the Green Queen, the Queen of May, and yes, the Green Witch by those who know no better. I am familiar with that sword. I know its name, and its origin. And I know something of its future. It is a terrible weapon that I hoped never to see in the hand of a man, though I knew that someday I would."

The depth of the sorrow in her voice drew me forward a step, but at my movement, she shrank from me. The wolves too started convulsively. Their fear seemed to energize the blade that shone of its own accord, but my heart reacted differently.

"My lady . . ." My voice sounded pleading to my own ears as I continued. "I do not wish to harm anyone or anything. Just reverse the spell that has taken the music from my village and promise to do no more dark magic, and I will leave you and yours in peace."

"How can I grant such a wish," she answered, "when I have performed no such spell. Indeed, the music that has been stolen was a treasure of my realm. It is not magic that has stolen the music; the music is magic that has itself been stolen. Listen, do you hear any music about you?"

I stopped then, immediately aware of the near silence that had followed me all day, and indeed since I entered the wild valley. Here, in the depths of a vast forest, not a bird sang, not a breeze whistled through the leaves. The Green Queen's voice, indeed, had a musical quality to it, but it was subdued and distant, like the echo of a song.

"You have captured it then, entombed it in some place and by some spell."

"I tell you," replied the Queen of May, "it is not some stroke of magic that has taken away the music. The music itself is magic, and it is the magic that has been stolen, though not by me. Magic is what animates my realm. The loss of music is a great loss to my power."

"Then who has stolen the magic?" I asked.

"Do you not know? Who would animate the world without magic, and thus would see magic as a rival?"

I thought back to the moving statues of knights, row upon row of them, which moved, not by magic, but by huge wheels and long beams. I pictured the straight stone walls and the enormous gates behind which the White Lady lived.

"Why would she send me to destroy you? What cares she in her castle of stone what you do here in the wood?"

"The existence of my realm is a challenge to her power. People believe in magic—many forms of magic, in fact, even if they do not call it such. She believes in a different power, and power is based on belief. She must destroy my realm for her power to reign supreme."

"What power does she wield? Is it not just another magic?"

The Queen of May was silent then for a while, lost in thoughts that were her own.

"No, though it may seem more like magic than much of the magic in the world, her power lacks mystery. It is bold and obvious and lifeless. I will say no more of that."

The reflection seemed to take a great deal out of her, and her shoulders slumped. The melancholy that had brought the wolves themselves to tears returned to her face, and she was beyond lovely. When I spoke again, I did so softly, carefully, beseeching answers but afraid of her reaction.

"But the healing woman in my village said that you had cast a spell on the girl and had stolen the music. She said that you practice dark magic."

"Dark magic?" the Queen of May replied, looking up, a little startled. "What is dark magic, and what makes it different from other magic?

Trees spring from the Earth, and from the tiniest acorn grows the greatest oak. That, surely, is magic, but is it dark magic? Birds return each year over thousands of leagues to the very trees from which they were hatched. Does dark magic lead them?"

"But she is a practitioner herself. Why would she fear your magic?"

The Queen of May laughed now, a trilling, crystalline laugh that warmed my heart—like spring after winter, it came to drive out the sorrowfulness that had settled over her just moments before.

"Why does she fear? You might just as easily ask why fish swim. Do you think that her tiny knowledge of magic makes her immune to fear? She fears because she has seen a glimpse, and dares not look farther. She uses what magic she may turn to her purpose with her eyes closed tight and her mind even more so. She seeks to use magic, so she sees only its power. If she were to seek to understand magic, she might come to embrace it, but it will not come to pass. My realm shrinks; there are few to walk open-eyed amid the magic that is all around us, so there are fewer and fewer to believe. Power requires belief," she said.

"The people believe in you," I whispered. She smiled warmly.

"They believe enough to fear. Even the White Lady believes, and so she has sent you and not come herself."

She reached out and laid a few fingers along the flat of the sword and raised the point to her breast.

"I believe in you, in your power. Your magic is the truth of your heart. If you think the world to be a better place without me in it, press your sword to its goal and finish your quest right here."

The world had faded away. The beasts of the wood had shrunk back, and even my loyal horse had wandered away, as if purposefully giving us room to converse. The world hung on the point of my sword. The blade trembled of its own intent, begging to be thrust home, but now my arm no longer faltered; my heart was no longer in turmoil. I dropped the sword to the ground and bent my knee to the ground. I felt a soft caress on the top of my head, an absent stroking of comfort and affection.

"Arise, Sir Knight," the Queen of May commanded, and the command was gentle and warm. "Your quest is not complete, for there is one in your village you must yet save, and the loss of music is spreading. Many fine things will be diminished if you fail. You must confront the White Lady, and wrest from her what magic she holds imprisoned. Yours is a hazardous path, but I may aid you yet.

"The magic is life, and life is magic. Therefore, the music will be imprisoned in a living thing. Find the creature that is held fast and you will find the prison. The White Lady has taken to herself many powerful tokens that she fears to use, for her future lies beyond the reach of magic, and using magic will not advance her hopes. But if she is desperate she will use whatever is at hand, and she has the strength and knowledge to wield great power.

"Within her stronghold is a knife, used for centuries by the wise and learned to cut the mistletoe from the oak. The mistletoe holds power, for it grows without ever touching the ground. It raises life above the stony Earth and brings it closer to the stars. The knife, too, must never touch the ground. The White Lady tricked one of the wise ones, and so gained possession of the knife. With it, she has ensnared many more of the wise. Free it, if you can, and bring it back to this sacred forest. But beware, the knife separates life from life, and makes a wound that will never heal. It is a great magic, and its use is fraught with peril."

At that, she looked up into the branches and her whole being seemed transformed. Where once stood a serious and stern lady, a queen to her very core, now there stood once again a girl as carefree as a spring breeze.

"Look," she cried, "the hummingbirds have come. Are they not the most beautiful of creatures?"

I could not say it then—indeed I was entirely mute in my astonishment—but I wished to contradict her. She herself was the most beautiful creature who ever walked the green paths of the world.

Chapter Ten:
A New Magic

The next morning I was saddled up again and off down the path that led past my village and up into the hills. I was grateful for the long, dull ride, for I needed to clear my head. The all-too-few hours I had spent in the realm of the Queen of May had been spent drinking up the sight of her, listening to her joyful prattling about the wild creatures that seemed drawn to her glen, as much from her kind and graceful manner as her surpassingly delicate beauty. I would gladly have floated forever there in the calm seas of her wooded kingdom.

Still, there was a task yet before me, and I had come to understand that my quest would affect more than a charming girl in my village and a few songbirds. The Green Queen had shown me the magic that flowed through every living creature, had brought me to understand that magic drew all living things together, and flowed between them in waves that nourished both the giver and the receiver. Ultimately, all the inhabitants of this world fed all the others, as the magic flowed through each and on to the ends of the Earth. Now a piece of that magic was gone, and many connections were broken. Music, it seemed, connected so many living creatures, and the lifeless objects that had spirits of their own as well. I felt my youth acutely then as I had never felt it before. The challenge seemed too much for one as inexperienced as I, and yet the Queen of May herself had sent me forth from the green wood, and I must try with all my strength and all my life to fulfill my charge.

My enemy, I had found out, was so far beyond me that I could hold no hope of success. She was a sorceress, who like the Green Queen herself commanded the magic that had brought forth the first green sprig. But the White Lady had mastered a new magic, one that did not flow between the creatures of the world, but divided and isolated them, and kept each in its place. It was a magic of separation and rules, of enforced order and control, and its wielder could exercise dominion in a way the old magic could not.

"Observe," the Queen of May had instructed, "how there are no living things within her castle walls. No trees, no plants, even the insects do not go there. Life has been pressed away, for life is connection and randomness and disorder. Even the grass that grows before her gates is ordered and grows where she wills it, not where the grass wills to grow. That influence is spreading. It has reached as far as your village. The healing woman is in her thrall; she practices her arts only so far as the White Lady allows."

"How far will it spread?" I asked.

"As far as it is allowed and as far as her servants can make it spread. Magic is belief, and so long as people believe that the world should be a place of order, that there are walls between living creatures, and rules that separate them, this new magic will prevail."

"Why take the music?"

"Do you not see? Music is a connection, it flows between one person and another, between one creature and another, between the wind and the water and the leaves on the trees. It is the purest form of the old magic there is."

This had given me pause, and I reflected on it for many hours as I traveled the wild lands. It was the last thought that ran through my mind as I fell asleep under the stars that night, but the first thought when I awoke was of the lady in green. As I saddled my horse and dismantled my little camp, I could not shake the feeling that she had been there beside me, just before I had opened my eyes.

Such reveries quickly disappeared as I became aware that the terrain was changing. The trees thinned and disappeared, and cold, dead rock began to dominate the landscape. I looked at this rock differently now. The Queen of May had explained that rocks too could be filled with magic. Rock that was still connected with the Earth, or that formed a home for living creatures or a foundation for growing mosses, was a part of the flow of magic. But these rocks were dead, broken, and scattered across an empty land. I felt the absence of life more keenly than I ever had.

As I approached the White Lady's castle again, I looked more closely at the grass that grew before its gates. I had once seen it as grass like all the rest, but I saw now how different it was. It was short and full, as if each blade had its place and each place had its blade. All the blades were grown to the same height, as if an invisible ceiling blocked any further growth. This grass grew, but it did not really live. I tried to imagine a village where the people lived in such dense order, and where everyone grew to the same height and no taller. The thought made me shiver despite the warmth of the spring sun.

Now I saw the path that led to the great white gates, and I remembered the grooves that brought the moving statue of a knight on his assault days before. A new knight stood at the gates, far ahead, though it looked indistinguishable from the one that had been there before. As I came to the start of the path, the knight's lance lowered into position. I urged my horse forward, and the knight charged.

I had no lance now—mine had been shattered in the earlier battle—but I had no intention of meeting my foe in a battle of honor. This was no knight of flesh and bone, and it was only the assumption that any opponent would fight fairly that made him so dangerous. As the knight approached, I kicked my horse into a sideways leap, and at the same time swung my sword, the marvelous, light, gleaming Sword of Days to Come, and cut the figure in two. The torso fell to the ground, and the rest of the knight and its horse continued on.

Unbalanced now, the knight toppled over as soon as it reached the end of the path. Immediately, the gates opened long enough for a new knight to take up its place, and then the ground closed again. Apparently I was still close enough to the path for whatever triggered these knights, and it charged straight away. I crossed the path just before it, ducking low beneath its lance and slicing the horse's front legs out from underneath.

This time the horse and knight crumpled right there, and as I started to ride wide of the path to avoid the inevitable next attack, the helmet of the knight flew off and landed before me, saving me from a terrible fate. Where the helmet touched the ground, the Earth seemed to leap upward with a terrific noise. A light brighter than any fire flashed before me, and earth flew in all directions. A rock that was kicked up in the tumult landed some three rods away and a similar bang ensued. Burning cinders filled the air, and wherever they landed on the shattered statues of knights, flames leapt into the air.

My terrified horse reared, nearly toppling me to the ground, where I suspect I would have been caught in another sudden blaze and killed on the spot. I hung on, and somehow kept my horse from bolting into the very danger he now feared. I was temporarily frozen, unsure where to turn, and realized that the gate was closing, another knight lowering his lance. I jerked the reins and spun my horse behind the crumpled remains of the last knight, just as the new one struck with such force that pieces of both knights flew about, setting off flashes whenever they landed more than a rod or two from the path.

I was ready now, and spurred my horse forward, blazing down the path with all the speed I could coax from him. We brushed by the emerging knight and slipped between the closing gates just as the new knight was launched. I heard the crash of the knight into the growing pile of debris, and the short, sharp blasts of the exploding earth, just before the gates clicked shut behind me. I was back in the courtyard of the stone castle.

Chapter Eleven:
The Wrath
of the White Lady

I leapt from my horse and led him along the inside edge of the gate, stepping cautiously around the grooves in the ground, but the knights arrayed against me made no move. Apparently they were animated only to guard the front gate. After circling around them, I found myself facing the inner wall of limed-white stone, the height of three men tall and to all appearances unbroken by any doorway. I stood baffled and defeated. I had achieved this first goal, but could go no further.

I should have anticipated this, but I was young and not yet skilled in seeing a path through the future. When I had last come to this castle, the White Lady herself had opened a passage through the wall with no markings on this side. How to make her do so again? And what would come forth if the gate did open?

As if in answer to my thoughts, the crystalline voice that seemed to come from all directions at once filled the air.

"You have returned. Have you vanquished the scourge in the woods?"

A voice inside my head said to lie, and to do so quickly, but my hesitation betrayed me.

"You have not, yet you have come back and destroyed many of my knights. She has bewitched you."

My ears had detected the voice coming more strongly from a spot not far to my right. I had to hear it again to be sure, so I tried to engage the voice.

"Why did you send your knights to attack me? Did I not leave here as a friend?"

There was a moment's hesitation. I held my breath, fearful that she had left me to stare at this blank wall. Then the voice rang out proudly.

"I see far, and knew you had come back to assault my castle. The dark magic radiates from you."

I focused on the place where the sound was strongest and began inching toward it. I had to keep the White Lady speaking.

"Then why ask if I had destroyed her, if you see so clearly?"

The response came in a suppressed hiss.

"How dare you, son of a dog? You must learn your place. It is the infection of that uncivilized harlot that has muddled your brains and made you forget that you are the nominal leader of a pack of mangy peasants. Perhaps I must clear your head!"

I leapt for the spot in the wall and found, flush with the stone and painted white, the end of a clay pipe. There must have been similar pipes all around the courtyard to create the effect of her voice. The White Lady's final words were still vibrating in the clay, and the threat in them was apparent. I pulled my sword from its sheath and thrust it into the pipe. When I twisted the hilt, the blade crashed through the clay and caught on the back of a stone.

Just at that moment, I heard stone grinding on dirt, and I looked up to see the gate in the hall begin to swing open. I thought for a second of pulling out my sword and racing for the gate, but thought better of it. From the gate emerged a wagon rolling on eight wheels, twice my height and as wide as a two-horse stable. But no horse pulled this wagon; some magic pushed it forward, and it wasn't the magic of the green wood.

Black smoke poured from a huge kettle atop the wagon, and tongues of fire shot up all around it. A terrifying whistle rent the air and made my ears sting and my eyes bulge. Most frightening, though, were the blades that came from every side of the wagon. They were curved like the swords that came from the southern lands, but they were longer by far than any spear shaft. They flashed in the sun, and I knew instantly that they were made of the same glorious material as the Sword of Days to Come.

As the wagon rolled from the gate, the blades flew in arcs and circles, slicing the very air all about. My horse gave a whinny of fright and bolted away across the courtyard, hiding himself among the unmoving knights. It looked like a good idea. Approaching the wagon would mean instant death, but I still had a task to complete.

I turned back to my original plan and levered the sword inside the hole in the wall. I feared that the blade would break, but the light metal seemed incomprehensibly strong. The stone began to give way, crumbling on the edge of the blade. I looked back over my shoulder and saw the wagon, amid a cloud of twirling blades, making a shallow arc and starting to come toward me. I thought about giving up and making for the outside gate, but a second wagon was already emerging from the gate in the inner wall, and it was swinging wide of the first. I wondered if there were more to come. I turned back and threw my weight against the hilt of the sword.

The stone below the hole in the wall cracked. I pressed again, and the stone split. Pieces began to fall away. The whistling was getting louder in my ears; the smoke was reaching my nostrils. I willed myself to not look back, and I set the blade against another stone. This one gave more easily, no longer supported by the crumbled stone beside it. In a moment the second stone was gone, and then a third. I dove through the hole I had made just before the first blade from the wagon clinked on stone.

Inside the inner wall, I found myself in a large reception hall, every bit as large as the one in the lord's castle. Dim light filtered in through a few high windows, but the room had all the appearance of dusk, despite it being full day. The whining screech of the wagon outside was mixed with the sharp clinking of blade on stone. Pieces of rock and dust filled the air, but the wagon was simply chopping away at the outside of the wall, and it would be a long time before it could cut its way through so many feet of stone.

I had other things to fear, though. Standing not twenty paces before me, staring into a huge crystal suspended from the roof, was the White Lady herself. Near her face was one end of a clay pipe, which rose and separated into many arms that ran along the wall in all directions. There were gears and levers all along the inside of the wall. No one else was about, and it dawned on me that there probably were no other people in the castle. The White Lady was directing her defenses, sending her wood and metal soldiers about, and opening gates all by herself.

She turned to stare at me, disbelief apparent in her eyes. It flashed through my mind that this must be the way I looked when in the presence of some magical event. Then her face went hard and she stepped toward me. At that moment, a most unusual thing drew both of our stares. Drifting through one of the small windows set in the ceiling came a brightly colored hummingbird, flitting about as if unconcerned with whatever was happening until it came to rest on my right shoulder.

The sight of the bird seemed to infuriate the White Lady, for she sent a small object, the size and shape of a children's top, flying up to where the bird sat on my shoulder. I heard the word "jump" whispered quietly but clearly in my ear, and I reacted to the sound. I leapt clear of the spot, the hummingbird flying in the opposite direction, just as the object exploded in a flash of light. Searing heat shot through my shoulder and along my cheek. I felt the heat enter my eye and burrow into it like a vengeful animal. My eyelid closed, covering an eye that would never see again. With my one remaining eye I saw that the White Lady was making another toss. To my amazement and relief, though, she was aiming at the hummingbird.

The bird easily flittered away from the second blast, and before the White Lady could let loose another throw, I had scrambled forward and pulled a foot from under her. She fell in a heap, the last of the flying fire pieces rolling out of her hand and going off harmlessly on the ground. I pulled myself up to my feet, still smarting from the first blast, and drew the Sword of Days to Come. The hummingbird settled back on my shoulder.

"I command the magic of the sword! It cannot harm me." Her voice was loud, but just a bit unsteady. The look in her eyes gave her away. It was a lie; she was afraid. I took a step forward, raising the sword.

"Give me what I want and I will not harm you, even though I have good reason to. I only want the magic that you have stolen returned . . . all of it."

Fear and indecision battled in her features. Her eyes glanced at a shrouded object a few feet away. It was a dome covered in cloth, sitting on a small table. A cage? A birdcage? A birdcage! As I reached out to grab at the cloth, something in the White Lady's hand flashed. A cold, sharp pain shot through my hand, and I watched as two of my fingers and a portion of my palm simply fell to the ground. The knife she had thrown sank into a wooden beam behind me.

I was staring dully at my mangled hand, the wound as straight and clean as if it were made by an ax, blood pouring from it. I barely registered the fact that the White Lady had leapt to her feet and run back along the wall toward the hole that I had made. She reached for a lever, gave it a tug, and then turned to stare at me with satisfaction. A section of the wall between her and me began to swing open. Another gate! She would let the sword-wielding wagons come in and trap me, and I was as good as dead.

But the creaking of stone as it slid across ground was quickly overtaken by another noise, the whining of the wagon itself growing louder and more shrill. The White Lady looked back in confusion, and the sound became unbearable. The front of the wagon appeared in the half-open door, and stopped moving forward. The flying blades had caught in the stone, fitfully loosening themselves for another arc and catching themselves again. With each grinding halt of the blades, the whining of the monster increased. The high-pitched whistle became a scream, a torrent of noise, and then ended in a deafening roar. A bright orange flame seemed to engulf the entire wall. Stone flew in all directions, and the ceiling above that half of the castle collapsed. The wagon had erupted.

The first bang was followed by a second, more distant and nearly lost in the roar of falling timber and splitting stone. I was far enough away not to be in the way of falling debris, but the blast sent me reeling. The White Lady was not to be seen through the flying dust. I scrambled to the shrouded cage, the Sword of Days to Come in one hand, the other hand, still bleeding profusely, pressed protectively to my chest. I set the sword down and gently lifted the black cloth.

Inside was a most remarkable creature, a mockingbird entirely golden in color, radiating light from within as soon as the cloth was removed. When the first shaft of light filtered through the dusty air and fell upon it, the bird began to sing. It was music of such a surpassing quality that it hardly seemed to belong to this world. The music did not just waft into the air and disperse; it hung about palpably. It had weight. It filled the room in ever-increasing density until I felt I was walking through liquid music.

I looked about for the hummingbird to see its reaction to the music, but I saw it looking sadly down at a bone-handled knife that lay on the ground beside a wooden post, uncaring of the music in the air. It was the knife the White Lady had thrown, the one that sliced off my fingers. I could only guess that it had fallen from the beam to the ground when the building shook. It was then, when I saw the hummingbird's mournful gaze, that I realized this was the knife of the wise people, the one that would lose its magic if it ever touched the ground.

I could not stand to look upon the obvious sadness of the little hummingbird, so I went instead to the pile of rubble to see what had become of the White Lady. She lay half buried in splintered rock and wood, covered in dust and unmoving. I thought she was dead until I heard a heard a faint cry escape her. I knelt down and took her head in my hands, and she opened her eyes. There was no light in them now; they were already going dim, but they focused briefly on me.

"Fool," she whispered, "you do not know as I do what is to come. I have seen the future, and it will be ruled by soldiers that are made, not born. There will be Earth that turns to fire, and metal things on wheels that will roll over all that oppose them. There will be birds of wood and metal that fly above and rain down fire. Men will live their lives chained in place, as much a part of these metal beasts as any rod of metal. You have defeated me, but you cannot defeat time."

"But why steal music from the land? What has that to do with these terrors?" I asked.

"I hoped . . ." she began, coughing pitifully. "I hoped to turn the minds of the people away from magic. Magic has no future. In the world to come, those who wield these new powers will rule all, will rule with an absolute authority that the kings of our day could not dream of. We must command this new power. Must . . . help . . . must make . . . them see . . ." And with that she closed her eyes and breathed no more.

Chapter Twelve:
Journey Back
to the Green Wood

I wrapped the knife in a cloth and stowed it inside my cloak. I let the mockingbird out of the cage, and it sprang forth into the air with a song that might have actually been more joyous than the one it had sung before. To my amazement, though, it did not fly away, but flew about me in a wide circle. I paused for a moment above the figure of the White Lady. She had been coldly beautiful in her own way in life, but the softening of her features in death made them more lovely, more gentle. I laid the Sword of Days to Come across her breast and walked out through the gate.

The courtyard of the castle looked like a battlefield. Pieces of wood and metal lay scattered about, and the charred markings of a fast-moving fire radiated across the ground. The explosion of the two wagons had engulfed the knights that had toppled, shattered, and burned. The huge wheels that had once moved the knights were a tangled heap of rubbish.

I found my horse shivering in a far corner of the courtyard, and the look of relief when he saw me was almost human. He stepped forward and nuzzled my neck and whinnied softly. I managed to climb up on his back, but the loss of blood from my wounded hand was quickly affecting my thoughts. If the gate were not constructed so well as to swing open from a push on a lever, my horse would not have been able to butt it open with his head, and I might not have escaped.

Daylight was just starting to fail as I started down the path from the gates of the castle. A deeper gloom was starting to creep over my eyes. I remembered little of the ride through that first evening and night. I am sure I slept, hunched in my saddle. From time to time, I seemed to wake to the sound of the mockingbird's song by my ear. Once I saw, or maybe just dreamt that I saw, the hummingbird suspended in the air beside my horse's head. The horse cocked his head toward the bird, then turned down a side path that branched from the road. I slipped back into unconsciousness.

I was next aware of my horse coming to a stop, and through my cloud-covered eyes saw an open clearing in a wood. A voice from far away called to me, a voice full of sweetness and warmth, and I slid off the horse in the direction of the voice. My head was cradled as I slipped to the ground, and I looked up to see the face of the Queen of May, more beautiful in its sorrow and concern than ever it was in the sunshine of a spring day. She took my injured hand in hers, heedless of the blood that still seemed to be flowing from the wound.

"This wound was made by the knife of the wise," she said with sorrowful surety. "It will never heal."

"Then I will feel blessed that I die with your face before me," I whispered, and I have never spoken any words with more truth. But the Green Queen put her fingers to my lips and shook her head.

"You are not going to die, my love, not tonight. Only put your trust in me."

She gave a low whistle, and one of the wolves came to her side, obedient as any hound. She placed one of her hands over my heart, and with the other held out my wounded hand before the wolf. Tears began to fall from her eyes, and I watched them fall, rather than see the wolf's jaws close on my hand above the wound. Then I knew no more.

When I awoke again, the sun was shining through the leaves and into the glen. The Queen of May knelt beside me, spooning little trickles of water through my lips. My hand was wrapped in

"*She held out my wounded hand before the wolf.*"

green leaves and, though sore, seemed to be cold and distinct, as if it were not quite attached to me. The lady in green said that she had been forced to make a new wound, one that would heal. She had soaked my hand in a poultice, and it was healing in its living bandage.

"It was a fearful wound, made by an instrument that was never intended to be used on living flesh."

Then the memory of the hummingbird staring sadly down at the fallen knife came back to me.

"The knife," I stammered "It fell, I couldn't help it . . . "

"Shh," the lady said, "I know, and you must not worry yourself about it."

How could she know? I asked myself. She must not understand.

"But the magic, it is gone."

"No," she smiled weakly, "it is not gone. Magic does not simply disappear, but it is scattered, and much of the good of it will be lost, but that is the way of all magic. And the White Lady has done much to diminish the magic in the world. She has fostered much disbelief, and where she failed at that, she has used belief to instill fear, and that cannot be undone. There will be others, too, who will work to rid the world of magic, driven by fear, or greed, or folly."

"And her visions? The White Lady said she could see the future, one without magic."

At this, the Green Queen looked grave.

"Her visions were true. The White Lady was a great sorceress, and she could indeed see far, as she claimed. There will indeed be a world where people will believe only in what they can see and what they can control, and so they will seek more and more to control others. But the White Lady did not see all, and she did not see to the end. Magic will always survive, even if it must hide in the deserted places of the world, and the unseen places in the minds of men.

"This forest, which houses and nourishes my own magic, will be cut down tree by tree, and someday the magic of the trees will be lost. I too will diminish and fade, for the magic that flows through me flows through the trees. But thanks to you, that day will be farther off, and some magic may yet remain in the realms of men that might have been scattered afar. You have done well, my Sapphire Knight."

She leaned down and kissed me, and the sweet taste of that kiss lingered on my lips for many a long day to come.

"The music?" I asked. "It was in the mockingbird?"

Now she smiled widely and freely, like a flower opening in spring.

"Yes, and you have set it free. See, it is here. It always comes back to look upon you as you rest."

She raised her hand, and from a tree nearby the mockingbird flew down and landed on my chest. It looked up into my face, opened its beak, and sang. Much of the golden color had faded, leaving a rather ordinary-looking bird, but the eyes still flashed gold. I looked up at the Green Lady questioningly.

"Oh," she said, "he has been over much of the land, spreading the music. The enchantment is nearly worn off."

"And the village girl?"

"As bright and songful as ever."

I sighed and settled back and slept again, deeply and peacefully.

Chapter Thirteen:
A New Dawn

The old man looked as if he had indeed fallen asleep in the telling, just as he had fallen asleep in the tale. His head drooped on his chest, his voice trailed off. I realized that I had not moved, indeed I might not have breathed, during the hours that the story flowed from him. He couldn't stop now!

"Old man," I nearly shouted, "what happened next? Did you wed the Queen of the Wood? Did you live with her in her realm? Did you really save the magic? Tell me."

His head bobbed only slightly; he was already far away. For a second, his one good eye opened wide and stared up into the horizon. A look of rapture engulfed his face, smoothing out wrinkles and covering scars and revealing the visage of a proud and comely youth at the height of his strength. And then his body slumped.

The firelight was dying, but a shimmer of light from the horizon heralded the coming of the dawn. For a second, darkness hung suspended between the two lights, and the air itself seemed to glow lightly from within. From the point on the horizon where he had looked, there came the flutter of wings. A small hummingbird flew down, hovered in the air, and then came to rest on the old man's shoulder.

The light, I'm sure, was befuddling my eyes. Shadows tell lies, and my eyes, enchanted by a wonderful story, believed them. For a flicker I saw the most beautiful woman that ever walked the paths of this world. She was dressed in shimmering green from the crown of ivy that encircled her head to the silk slippers that adorned her feet. Her hair was the color of gold; her eyes shone a sapphire blue. She laid a hand gently along the old man's face, cradling the scarred and useless eye, and kissed him gently on the lips. Then the sun rose above the horizon, the shadows fled, and I was left with only the lifeless form of the old storyteller.

That was the night I became a bard. I would tell stories, I told myself, because I have to tell this one. I make no claim that it is true; I only give to you what he gave to me. I will never tell it as well as he did, but it is a story that must be told, and now I have.

Epilogue:
The Song of the Sapphire Knight

*Honor me, oh lady proud, and
Deign to be my love, the captain
Of my heart. For you are green
And I am blue. You are grass
Bespeckled of the dew,
Always growing, ever in bloom
And I am the ever moving,
Never changing
Stony cold of the sea.
I am blue, so very cold
The depth of winter when all
To a stand have come.
Yet to come to you, to spring
To green from blue
One need only add
The yellow of the sun.*

123

About the Author

Michael Sullivan is a storyteller, juggler, chess instructor, librarian, and a former school teacher who grew up in small town New Hampshire, and now lives in Portsmouth, NH. He has worked with kids in many settings, from summer camps to the Boston Museum of Science, and is rumored to have once been a kid himself. He is the author of the book *Connecting Boys With Books*, and speaks across the country on the topic of boys and reading. In 1998, he was chosen New Hampshire Librarian of the Year.

Visit Michael's website at:
www.talestoldtall.com/BoyMeetsBook.html